MY QUESTIONS TO LIFE

QUESTIONS I ASK MYSELF, AND SO SHOULD YOU...

MAHEK TRIVEDI

ISBN 979-888606449-0

I am not someone who's master at everything that is written in this book I am the one who's learning everyday to master all of these ONE day and while I am on my journey, contemplating my life, learning from my experiences, I thought of writing it for anyone who might want to change their way of thinking and life too.

Contents

Preface *vii*

The Inception

1. Who Are You? 3
2. What Is I ? 5
3. What Is Karma According To You? 7

The Purpose

4. What Is The Purpose Of Life? 13
5. How Does The Law Of Karma Work? 15
6. Why Do Expectations Always Hurt? 18

The Resolution

7. Why Things Aren't Going The Way I Planned? 25
8. What To Do If I've Already Made Mistakes? 28
9. Blessed To Be Stressed? 31
10. How To Multiply Your Wealth Through The Right Ways? 35

Epilogue 39

Acknowledgement 41

Preface

Have you ever thought what you have been taught for years now, can be wrong? Your perspective towards your life, can be different from what's really life is? Do you have an ambiguous viewpoint on life? If you're open for a new change in your life then this is THE life changing book you need, even if you're 15, 22 or even 80.

I believe that everyone is an OMNISCIENT, you know it all, but where one lack is the ignorance of knowledge about one's self. There's no age limitation to know your own self.

My only motive behind this book is to open up your thinking capacity to infinity, the universe is infinite and so, consequently there can be infinite answers to one question.

Let's start this beautiful journey by beginning it today.

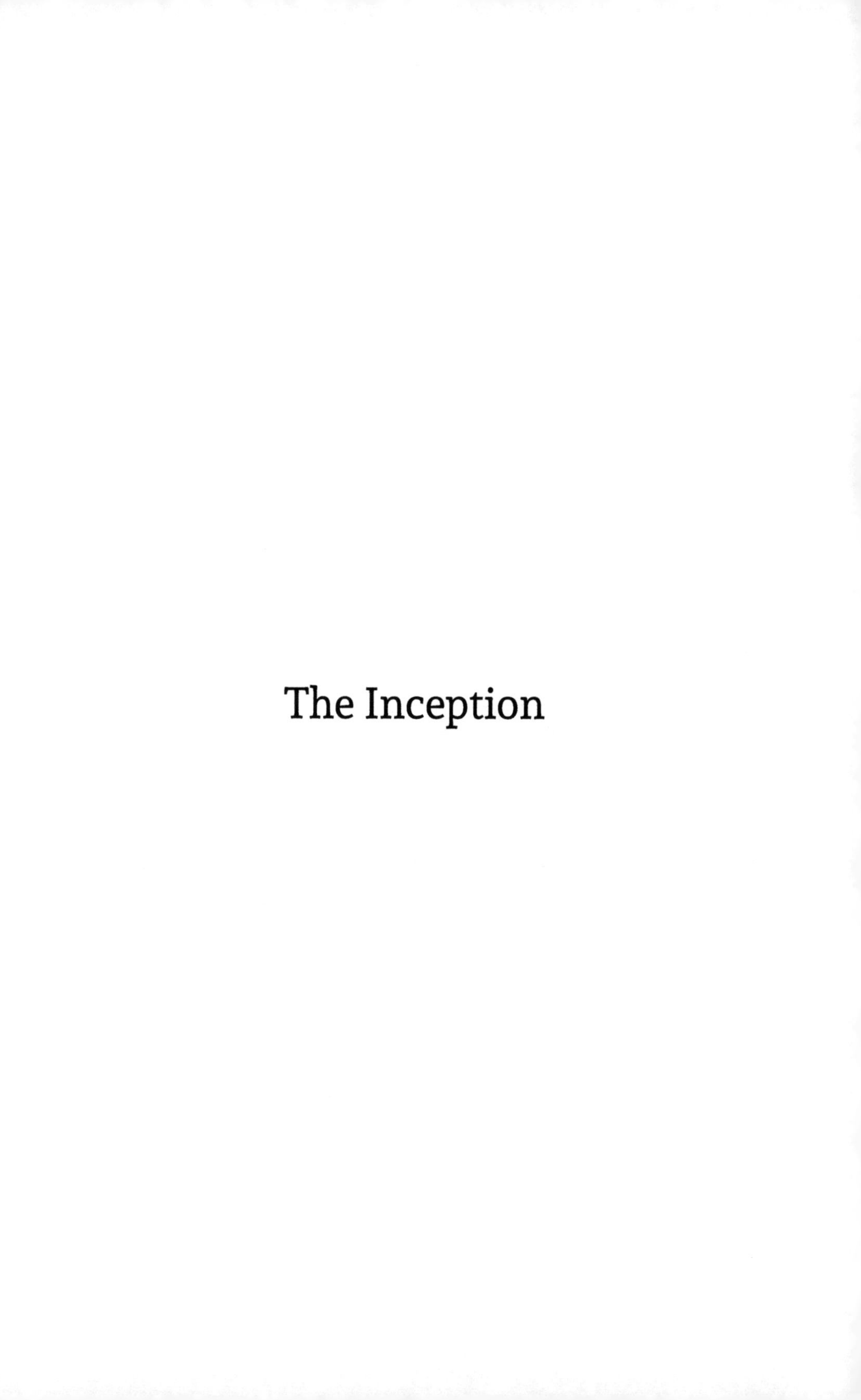

The Inception

ONE

WHO ARE YOU?

"This world is not at fault, the world is beautiful. If your understanding is wrong, what can the world do?"

- **Dadabhagwan**

ÞÞÞ

They say we all are children of Brahma, some say we are children of Jesus, some say Allah and many more names have been given since years. And on that basis, we all are given different dharma, some worship with folded hands some with open hands and we're taught to do certain things in certain ways only. But who created these things? Who are they? THEY ARE US. We created all these. Let me tell you one thing, I'm a Brahmin and Brahmins make many types of rules which were thought to be the best for the society for anyone and so, I'm not here complaining or degrading any type of religion but while growing up I realised that the rules which were made by our forefathers were for some other purpose and the rules which we follow are totally differently and conveniently mutated, however we prefer. I call it the "**opportunistic religion**" for example when women are in periods they should not touch or work during those days, as women are bleeding on those days constantly. The purpose behind this is to not make them work so that they can get proper rest. According to our "opportunistic religion", periods are considered impure, women cannot touch anything but can wash clothes. How can something that is natural, be impure? A soul neither bleeds nor it is the flesh, you misunderstood it by considering yourself, you're not this face, looks, colour of your skin, your gender, your caste, your religion.

You are your thoughts, your feelings, your actions, your passion, your emotions, your compassion, your guts & overall a SOUL. And a soul is always PURE. So, you are a pure soul, that's it.

But due to the ignorance of that knowledge you think you are Mahek (your name) & from that, is where your karma starts. You think that Mahek is a doer, Mahek is eating, Mahek is thinking and in that way you cause a blunder between what you really are and Mahek. You make a huge mistake by considering yourself and your name as the same. Were you already given the name when you were born? No. Then who were you before the name was given to you? The name is just given to you as an identity. You are simply a pure soul, segregated from the universe / god / brahma whatever super power you believe, came into the world to experience life and then to go back to him again.

TWO
WHAT IS I ?

"Suppose, if all insects died today then approximately within 2 to 4 years all life on this planet will cease but if all the human beings died, the planet will flourish."

- **Sadhguru**

ϸϸϸ

Ego is the Latin word for I. I is simply your ego. Someone asks you to make tea, then they compliment you so obviously you will feel good, you will feel kind of superior that "I" made the tea. Your ego is satisfied. Now, go back to the time when you started making the tea, you took a vessel, poured some water, kept it on the stove, added sugar, tea etc... Now, can you answer a few questions here? Answer in yes or no. In the making of 'your' tea, have you made the vessel which you used? Have you made the sugar? The tea? Or the water? It's a circle. Someone planted the seeds for the tea, someone had to bring it to the wholesaler, then to the retailer then it came to you and only after that, you had the perfect tea you thought that "I" made. And it applies to every task, every work you do. Do analyse these things next time you expand your ego in the successful completion of your work. Ego is not who we really are. It is our social mask, the role we are playing. Your ego demands the need for approval and the need to control things.On who are you conceited of? Who are you impressing? Accept that reality, that you cannot always be good in everyone's story. Sometimes you are directly or indirectly bad or maybe worse in someone's story. According to Hindu mythology, Shri krishna was also bad from the kaurva's side because he didn't take their side, right?

(Excluding the fact that he sent his army with them, they still didn't like him) then who are you? If the god himself cannot be good in everyone's story how can you expect everyone to be happy with you all the time. You can try and make everyone happy as much as you can. But don't expect the respect or the appreciation in return not everyone will give you and it's not good for you too because that will make you believe that whenever you do anything it's always right and people will recognise it and appreciate you. You don't need that! As shree Krishna stated in Bhagwat Geeta

कर्मण्येवाधिकारस्ते मा फलेषु कदाचन । (Chapter 2, verse 47)

You have the right to perform your prescribed duties but you're never entitled with the fruits of your actions.

Even if you win or lose you must perform your actions being neutral, without expecting anything in return.

मा कर्मफलहेतुर्भूर्मा ते संगोऽस्त्वकर्मणि ॥ (Chapter 2, verse 47)

Never consider yourself to be the cause of the results of your activities and be attached to its action.

The reason is that our senses, mind, and intellect are ignited by a supreme power, it energizes us with its power and puts them at our disposal. So, only with the help of the power we receive from it, we are able to work.

So, tell me now, who made the good tea?

THREE

WHAT IS KARMA ACCORDING TO YOU?

"When people ask me how can you prove that it (karma) exists? My question to them is how can you prove that it doesn't exist?"

- **Ranveer Allahbadia (beerbiceps)**

There can be numerous answers for each question in this world. For example, If I ask you, do you believe in God's existence? Let us assume your answer as yes, but if I ask this same question to 4 more people I might get different perspectives about it. It's not about what you think you already know, it's about unlearning the wrong things and learning the right things. You should always be open to other's perspectives because you never know what you have been thinking/taught since years might be wrong?

Disclaimer:- Not your Instagram page's content

I asked a few people about what they think about karma, do they believe in the law of karma? What is karma, according to their point of view? I've got really great answers from some people and really instagramish (is that a word?) answers from some.

The word karma was found in the Rigveda. It is one of the four sacred canonical texts of Hinduism known as the Vedas and Bhagavad Gita is where karma first appears strongly. Karma is derived from the Sanskrit word kriya which means actions, whatever you do right from the minute you wake up from the bed to even when you're deep asleep in your dreams, everything we have ever spoken, thought, done or caused, is a karma. Have you heard of a child born with disorders? Have you seen labourers working hard everyday and getting little money? Have you ever heard of someone who never smoked a cigarette but still got lung cancer? Why? We have always been taught that do good and good will come back to you, then why is this all happening here? Why the poor are getting poorer by being loyal and honest & the rich getting richer by corruption, bribery, murders etc...? Let's take an example, two seeds were sown in the same place, at the same time, but one perished and the other flourished why? There can be many other elements like the water given, the nutrients, fertilizers, light, air quality, temperature etc... You think that you did good to someone and so good things should happen to you in the same form. But there are numerous factors which come into the play while determining your results. They can be your spirit (how you did it), your intentions (why you did it), your efforts (what energy you gave), the place, situation and the most important factors are your past karmas and cumulative karmas of the people involved with you. Yes, the intentions of the people with whom you're performing any task should be as pure as yours. As they say, it takes two to tango; if two people are involved in some work then if the work is not executed properly then it's the fault of both of the parties. Both of the person's intentions should match. Also, if you've done something wrong in the past and you're doing really great right now to do something good for yourself or for others but it's not happening, then it is your past Karma's mistakes which has led you here today. There's absolutely no one's fault in it.

Have you ever seen someone really rich taking his money, assets or even liabilities with him after dying? The only thing you'll be taking to your next life are your karmas. No one is taking these materialistic things, this fame, this name and not even these relations.

भगवान के घर देर है, अंधेर नही (there is delay in God's justice but it's never denied). There is neither delay nor justice is denied. It is as it should be. Whatever you're getting, you're getting at the exact right time at which you should. You are given this situation because you consciously or unconsciously you created this situation for you from your deeds. No god can do anything about it. Take responsibility for your own actions.

These are some of the beautiful answers that I got from people:

1. Univere's way to balancing things out. For some people it is the reason to do right things but for me it is a looped cycle which is always fair, even when you don't believe in it.

- **Sanskruti Patel**

2. Each action we create with physical and mental abilities, makes a memory. I think that's Karma.

- **Kanchi Sanghavi**

3. I believe Karma is God.

- **Parth Mehta**

4. Karma is like one's own responsibility, like a plant, the way we nourish it, it will bloom. We cannot blame anyone if our plant withers.

-**Krishal Badshah**

5. Every single thing you do is karma with respect to emotions and intentions attached.

-**Kavya Shah**

6. Karma is what you do, you get. If I've done something good today i will definitely get it back today or tomorrow. But you should have that patience to wait for it, which i think people don't understand it.

-**Bhargavi Mevada**

The Purpose

FOUR

WHAT IS THE PURPOSE OF LIFE?

"The best way to find yourself is to lose yourself in the service of others."

- **Mahatma Gandhi**

What is the first thing that came to your mind? It might be that I want to make my parents, kids happy/to marry the love of my life/to gain success in life by getting richer, etc. But what I'm asking is what is THE purpose of life and not the purpose of your "materialistic life". It is expected from us, the human beings, that we create something that is good for us as well as other lives because we are the only creatures who are blessed with the sense of thinking, speaking and understanding that's why humans are the most evolved creatures on earth. But with the evolving process he has forgotten how to live with peace, what he thinks about his purpose is to earn money, satisfy his & his family's needs, maintain a social status and that's all. Lord Mahavir says, **'Use your mind, speech, body and Soul (worldly self) for others. If then, you experience any pain, let me know.'**

Every living being, every soul who takes birth in a body, its purpose is to serve others with what they have without seeking for what's in for them. Have you ever seen a tree giving shade to other living beings and expecting or asking for something in return? What is the sun expecting from us? We as humans cut the trees when needed, curse the sun when there's too much rain and it's not showing up. That's why humans are called the most selfish creatures on the planet too. What we are doing is exactly the opposite of what our purpose truly is. We are expected to give as much as we can as & as much as we have, either be it any service or food or water or anything that we have. We are blessed with the most powerful thing which is "the brain", we're given the privilege to think about what's right and what's wrong. And how are we using it? By thinking that "I've done so much for them and when I needed them the most they were not there for me. I should stop being such a fool and help them." Being nice and humble and helpful to someone is regarded as stupidity in this society. It's high time to stop doing the wrong things and start doing the right things that are serving whatever and whoever and whenever we can. The ultimate purpose for human life is to attain moksha - what they say is, "the one who is born, must die." Where we are stuck is, by bounding ourselves with too much good, bad, regular, irregular karmas we're stuck in the worldly cycle of taking birth and dying. The main purpose of every soul is to attain moksha and for that one must stop behaving like he's a doer. In that way only, you can separate yourself from the Karmas and the results of karmas from you. That separation will eventually lead you to moksha.

FIVE

HOW DOES THE LAW OF KARMA WORK?

"I try to live with the idea that karma is a very real thing. So I put out what I want to get back."

- **Megan Fox**

ꝒꝒꝒ

You saved a dog's life in the morning and had chicken for dinner. Now tell me, how will the karma cycle work for you? Do you believe that you will not get punished for eating the chicken because you saved someone's life?

I was very curious about knowing the sin & virtues laws from my childhood, when I was around 13 and wasn't aware much about the karma thing, I witnessed a man throwing a stick on a cat who was about to eat a mouse. At that time, a question prompted in my head, will that man get the virtue of saving the rat's life or will he get the sin for hurting the cat?

Bhagwat Geeta has stated that no action of any man goes unnoticed and despite the superiority, the after effect will not get pacified. If we relate this to science, even Newton's third law states the same. So, if we take a closer look, Karmas are of 3 types..

1. Kriyaman karma:

Kriyaman karma also known as Vartaman karma. As the word suggests, these are the Karmas that we do in the present which is instantly completed and the fruit is given to you at that time only.

For example, you got hungry, you ate, you were satisfied, your action gets completed.

2. Sanchita karma:

Sanchita means to accumulate. Some of the actions which you execute, you get the results after sometime, that can be, after some hours, some months, some years or maybe in the other life. It is again, decided from the other factors too (which I've mentioned in the 3rd chapter). It is more or less like arrows in quiver as the good karma does not cancel the effect of bad one. Instead, they stay side by side and life goes on.

For example, You gave your exam today, you won't get the results at the same time right? You will get it after some days or months. Just like that some karmas you will perform today but you will get the results after a period of time.

3. Prarabdha karma:

It is related to the accumulated karmas and known as Discharged karmas. This type of karma is like an arrow that has already left the bow and is about to reach the destination. It can also relate to "the words, once spoken, cannot be taken back at any cost". When the Karmas are accumulated in this life, those karmas give fruits in the other life. Those karmas are then discharged and the fruits are given.

For example, You wanted to become an actor but due to various circumstances in your current life and your past karmas, you became an engineer in this life. So now, the present life's karmas becomes accumulated karma & in your next life, you take birth to become an actor and fulfill your karmas. Thus, your Accumulated karma of current life gets discharged in the next life.

The amount of or else, you can say the number of good as well as bad deeds that you've done are recorded in a book called, **"The Law Of Karma"**. Until one has a store of good deeds, then the bad deeds are forgiven. Whenever the good deed's quota is over then comes the bad deeds & that's different for different areas of life.

Let us understand in detail,

Your good deeds & bad deeds are categorised in various different areas like Money, Health, Relationship, Work, etc. Here, the bad deeds of one area does not set off against the good deeds of another area and vice-versa. Let's take an example: When we look at someone who's rich in monetary terms, big houses, numerous cars, luxurious life, we often think that he's so lucky that he has everything in life. But little do we know that he can't sleep at night until he takes his sleeping pills. He's enjoying his wealth because of his karma but at the same time, was also suffering mental health issues because of it.Here, the areas of karma were different. He must have done something good and worked hard to get that luxurious life, but he might have done something wrong to reach to that point of his life.

Now, you must have got the answer for my question that I had in the beginning, right? That man will get the sin for hurting someone as well as he will get the virtue of saving someone's life too. The karma cycle is so well established that it has no loopholes and no one can escape from any single karma.

According to our mythological tales, Lord Ram's father the king Dashrath was also destined to die without his favourite son because while hunting in the forest for the animals, he accidentally shot his arrow at a teenager boy named Shravan and his parents cursed Dashrath that he too would die without his son. Ram could've made some exceptions for his father. After all he's the lord himself, he could've just denied to live in the forest for 14 years, right? But that's what they teach us from these epics that when the lord takes birth as a human being, even he cannot escape from the law of karma. He accepted all that came to his path, we have to do the same. Accept whatever is coming and act accordingly.

Sahadev in Mahabharata, was blessed by the gods to see the future, but can we consider it as a blessing or as a curse?He knew everything that was going to happen. He could've saved his wife from all that happened, he could've stopped his brothers from playing the game, but could he? He must have tried to stop the war, but nothing worked right. I think knowing the future will only make you worry more about it and will not allow you to live in the present. The thing which we learn here is that even though knowing what is going to happen in the future you CANNOT stop it. What you've already sown, you will definitely get either it's good or bad, today or tomorrow, this life or next life.

We all create some or the other type of karma of which we'll have to suffer the consequences. You can pacify your karmas through akarmas. Akarmas means the actions performed without any desire for personal benefit and only for the service of others. So, keep this in mind that you cannot escape the karma that you have created and hence keep a check on your deeds without fail. However, you cannot get rid of the Karmas that you have already created but you can decrease its effects by doing certain practices. (which you will read in further chapter no.8)

SIX

WHY DO EXPECTATIONS ALWAYS HURT?

"*When you stop expecting people to be perfect, you can like them for who they are.*"

- Donald Miller

ᑭᑭᑭ

First, let us talk about desires. Some Desires give birth to some expectations. Desire — a strong feeling of wanting to have something or wishing for something to happen.

There can be 2 types of Desires. One, which gives pain and binds us to the world and the second that gives us joy and liberation.

Desires which give you short term of happiness and long-term of pain and sorrow are..

1. Desire to acquire more and more things — wealth, fame, position, name, respect, status, reputation, money, etc. The nature of these desires is such that when they get fulfilled, they give birth to new desires and if they are not fulfilled, they cause tremendous disappointments. One is never satisfied with what one has and never reaches a contentment level hence they're always in a mode of pain, sorrow, struggle, competition, comparison, judgements.

2. Desire to get free from pain, sorrows, adverse situations, bad luck, troubles and to get free from people who give pain and sorrows. It is mandatory that pain, sorrow, adverse situations will occur in life, because That's Life. Life is nothing without the ups and down. If you don't get the downs then how will you value your ups? If you're not moving you're not living.
3. Desire to always get favourable outcomes from all the efforts, actions, reactions, activities, expectations, karmas etc.. Here, we forget that a situation cannot always give results in the way we ONLY desire.

अगर कसिी चीज को दलि से चाहो तो पूरी कायनात उसे तुमसे मलिाने की कोशशि में लग जाती है।

When you want something, all the universe conspires in helping you to achieve it. -**Paulo Coelho**

Ya, this sounds very happening and feels confident, when you are feeling demotivated and when you're feeling short and it is true to a certain extent too, but regardless of how strongly we desire for a favorable result there is no guarantee of the same. As there is no rule that whatever we desire strongly will get fulfilled and at our desired time only. So, there is always a component of disappointment and sorrow in these desires.

Rather than we should desire of those desires which give happiness and liberation..

1. The desire to be desire-less. Where one is content with what one has and does not want to acquire anything more. In fact, one is grateful for whatever he has and uses the available resources for the upliftment of others.
2. Desire for everyone's happiness. One does not like, even enemies, to suffer in any way and prays for everybody's wellness, good health, success, growth and harmony.
3. Desire for enlightenment. The desire to get free from the cycle of karmas and birth, death and rebirth. One wants to know about the purpose of life and to get moksha. The desire to get moksha is considered to be the most ideal desire for a human being to have.

This does not mean that you should stop desiring everything you want to achieve and just focus on the last 3 desires. Instead, you should analyse your desire, know the outcomes and then decide your priorities.

The desire-world stops at a certain point. You desire something for a few days or a few weeks and then you give up. Beside that, expectation does not leave you. In a certain sense, expectation is more harmful in the spiritual life than desire.

You always expect from the people you're attached to. You don't expect from the one you aren't attached to. When the expectations are fulfilled more expectations occur & when it's not fulfilled then it causes some disliking and frustration for that person. "I've done so many things for that person, then why are they not giving me appreciation, why are they not valuing what I'm doing for them." But stop once and ask yourself, why are you doing those things for them? Did they ask you to do it? You're doing it out of YOUR attachment, because of your limerence. Just like Newton's 3rd law, for every action, there is an equal and opposite reaction. The deeper your limerence, the deeper would be your loathing for that person. Everytime you suffer, even if it's the smallest thing, think about it that what did I do that I'm suffering from? Don't start blaming the person for not fulfilling your desires & expectations. Your life is your deeds, nothing else. Anything you feel is the cause of your actions. No one is responsible for what you're facing and you're experiencing, you're the only one who created the life you're living. We often misinterpret situations and then hurt ourselves by thinking way too much about it. If you are to be with this person for a fixed period of time then even if you change the whole universe for them, that person won't come back again. Because, you're here (in this world) for a fixed period of time only. The day of your mortal death was already fixed on the day you were born. The body is mortal, the soul isn't. This is a hard truth that we all need to understand before it gets too late and we overthink the overthinking work. Just accept the fact, don't force the relationship, try and find where you lacked, then improvise yourself in that area & if you think that you did nothing wrong then just move on with the good memories you had with them. Why do you want to curse or cry about that person that left you? It's just that you had this much time together only. And let me tell you very wisely, that as that one person came and went there will be several other people who will come, stay, go, come back again.... And at the end of this circle, you will leave everyone and go to the other life, where you belong then. Read that again. And understand it. So, what impressions are you taking with yourself? Be careful about that. Keeping any kind of hate will connect that person to your other life (as explained in chapter 5) and that cycle will continue till you stop the overflow of love or hate for any person. Start finding the reasons behind your suffering/your unhappiness, with each and every person you're having the attachments with. It can be your parents, your partner, your children, your friends, your colleagues with anyone you have what expectations you have with them? Try and remove all those expectations one by one day after day, tell yourself that whatever you're doing is because of your limerence try to remove that, do things for others without expecting anything in return & you will get to live a boundless and a peaceful life.

The Resolution

SEVEN

WHY THINGS AREN'T GOING THE WAY I PLANNED?

"But if something did happen, it happened.

Whether it's right or wrong, I accept everything that happens, and that's how I became the person I am now."

- **Haruki Murakami**

ჶჶჶ

They say, whenever things are not going your way, they're going at the god's way. I will tell you to think positive about every situation, and you must have heard about these lines zillion times but I'm sorry to burst this myth to you that when things aren't going your way, they aren't going to the god's way too. They're going the exact right way which they should! How? When you've already done the Karmas where you've hurted someone, you've snatched from someone's plate & ate the bread then how can you expect that it will return to you in the other way? Again, the law of karma - what goes around, comes around. It will come to you in some other form but with the same intensity & with same feeling that the person felt. Whenever things aren't going your way, take a pause, look at the situation and think if you've done something like that to someone else? If yes, then you must recognise and try to ameliorate it. How? That you will learn in the next chapter. If not, then ask for the forgiveness of the deeds that you must've done in some other life.

You will NEVER get anything bad or wrong if you haven't done anything bad or wrong. The law of karma does not have loopholes. Everything – the good and bad, pleasure and pain, approval and disapproval, achievements and mistakes, fame and shame. Everything has a beginning and an ending and that's the way it's supposed to be.

The non-permanent appearance of happiness and distress, and their disappearance in due course, are like the appearance and disappearance of winter and summer seasons. They arise from sense perception and one must learn to tolerate them without being disturbed.

Once a king called upon all of his wise men and asked them, "is there a mantra or suggestion which works in every situation, in every circumstance, in every place and in every time. In every joy, every sorrow, every defeat and every victory? One answer for all questions? Something which can help me when none of you is available to advise me? Tell me is there any mantra"? All the wise men were puzzled by the King's question. After a lengthy discussion, an old man suggested something which appealed to all of them. They went to the king and gave him something written on paper, with a condition that the king should not see it out of curiosity. Only in extreme danger, when the King finds himself alone and there seems to be no way, only then he can see it. The King put the paper under his Diamond ring. Sometime later, a neighbouring king attacked the Kingdom. King and his army fought bravely but lost the battle. The King had to flee on his horse. The enemies were following him. And, they were getting closer and closer. Suddenly the King found himself standing at the dead end of the road - that road was not going anywhere. Underneath there was a rocky valley thousand feet deep. If he jumped into it, he would be finished and he could not return because it was a small road the sound of enemy's horses was approaching fast. The King became restless. There seemed to be no way. Then suddenly he saw the Diamond in his ring shined in the sun, and he remembered the message hidden in the ring. He opened the diamond and read the message. The message was "THIS TOO SHALL PASS".The King read it. Suddenly something struck him- "Yes! This too will pass. Only a few days ago, I was enjoying my kingdom. I was the mightiest of all the King. Yet today, the Kingdom and all my pleasure have gone. I am here trying to escape from enemies. Like those days of luxuries have gone, this day of danger too will pass." A calm came on his face. He kept standing there. The place where he was standing was full of natural beauty. He had never known that such a beautiful place was also a part of his Kingdom. The revelation of the message had a great effect on him. He relaxed and forgot about those following him. After a few minutes he realized that the noise of the horses and the enemy coming was receding. They moved into some other part of the mountains. The King was very brave. He reorganized his army and fought again. He defeated the enemy and regained his empire. When he returned to his empire after victory, he was received with much fanfare. The whole capital was rejoicing in the victory. Everyone was in a festive mood. Flowers were being showered on King from every house, from every corner. People were dancing and singing. For a moment King said to himself. "I am one of the bravest and greatest Kings. It is not easy to defeat me." With all the reception and celebration he saw an ego emerging in him. Suddenly the Diamond of his ring flashed in the sunlight and reminded him of the message. He opened it and read it again: THIS TOO SHALL PASS. He became silent. His face went through a total change from the egoist he moved to a state of utter humbleness.

So, whenever you're confronted with these types of situations and challenges where you feel the most deteriorated and cannot find out the reason, also in the situations where you feel like you're on cloud nine and everything is happy and going well, remind yourself "This too shall pass". By telling yourself this sentence you ask your brain to think of another possible outcome i.e if you're in some bad situation, tell him, this is not how it's going to be the same your whole life, cheer up, get up and do your work. When you're too much happy, you feel transcending & conquered, tell him, that moment is also not going to be the same, so don't get egotist and feel superior if you're winning at something, today you're winning them, tomorrow you might lose and vice versa. This is how life is. There is nothing permanent in this world, **EVERYTHING changes, EXCEPT the law of change**. Think over it from your own perspective. You have must have exprienced all the changes. You have survived all setbacks, all defeats and all sorrows. Everything have passed away. The problems in the present, they too will pass away, because nothing remains forever. And if everything passes by then you're just a watcher, nothing is yours, we all are witnesses of all what's coming and going... So, what's yours is really not yours and what you want is not what you really need.

EIGHT

WHAT TO DO IF I'VE ALREADY MADE MISTAKES?

"Seeing others' faults is indeed an echo of our own fault, the biggest fault is our own fault which is known as EGO."

- **Dadabhagwan**

Sometimes, knowingly or unknowingly you're placed in a situation where your karmas are repeated and there's a greater reason for that. It is to teach you to take different actions for different results. If you're attracting the same type of partners or people into your life over and over again, it's time to stop and inspect your choices: Why do similar people keep coming in? What should you be doing differently? This calls for an honest introspection and evaluation of your own faults and weaknesses, which is admittedly hard to do. Don't be afraid to look within. Recognize what must be changed inside of you so as to change what's outside of you. Because as they say, until you don't learn your lesson from one particular thing you will often be placed in those type of situations.

Now, this is something what I've been doing since years and for me, it works like magic. If you also want to try then it's totally harmless. What is already done cannot be changed now, but the damage which is caused can surely be sorted out.

There are 3 ways through which you can ameliorate your mistakes.

1. Evaluation:-

Recalling your mistakes. i.e recognising where have you made the mistakes, to whom you were not good in this life, to whom you knowingly or unknowingly hurt their emotions.

2. Improvise:-

Just like the rectification entries you did in the accounts. You need to recognise the errors you made and rectify it. Try and ask for forgiveness to their soul, this might sound preposterous but I have a reason behind this too. We all are a part of the same universe, every soul is connected to each other either it's a dog or cat or a human being, the way you think and feel about them effects more than your words, as the vibrations (the vibes you call in slang) which you provide goes to other soul before your words and those vibrations creates your AURA. We all are connected through one energy which you can call Bhrama or Jesus or Allah or whatever you may. It is all one. We all are one. Pray really from the depth of your heart for forgiveness to that soul, remember every time you did wrong to that particular soul.

3. Assurance:-

To vow, 'I will never do that again. I promise that I shall not repeat the mistake again', is called Assurance. (here)

Ask for forgiveness and ask for strength to the god you believe in, to never hurt someone again, try and do this for every person you've met and you think you've done something wrong and you will certainly feel less burden.

It's not about your ego or who was wrong or right. It's about, do you want to get out of this never ending worldly cycle of hating, loving and hating again or not? Asking for forgiveness on their face might level up their ego or might deteriorate yours, right? Then try this method and tell me how you felt then. The second part of the coin, if someone did wrong to you. Forgive them for yourself, not for them. Because forgiving them will stop that anger and frustration and bad vibrations from your body. Even if they never asked for forgiveness, forgive them so that YOU can live a peaceful life. Look, life is too short to hold grudges. Do you even know the one with whom you're fighting and not talking right now is he/she going to live for years? What if they die tomorrow? (I don't wish that) but just have that thought in your mind for once and then see how suddenly you will change your mind and accept them with all of their flaws and mistakes right now. If you don't and if the person goes away from your life suddenly then you have to live with that repentance your whole life. Accept this fact that there's two side of a coin (exception case of sholay) if you think they did wrong to you then you must have done something wrong too. Either today or yesterday or maybe in any other life. No one can even pinch you without "you" being involved in that, before. This is how meticulously the law of karma works.

NINE

BLESSED TO BE STRESSED?

"*What people are suffering is not their bondage, what they're suffering is their freedom.*"

- **Sadhguru**

The only thing that you or your stressed body need is some time to just be alone & be in the present moment, to sit alone, gather your thoughts. Solitude is the key. No, I'm not talking about meditation, even though that's the ultimate motive of this exercise. To get started, just sit alone in a room full of light (never darkness, I repeat never), close your eyes & just observe your thoughts, what kind of thoughts you're having? Take notes of it (literally on a paper). Let your thoughts come naturally and make a note of which are the most common thoughts you're having.. Is it about your future? Your past? Your upcoming wedding? Your better half? Your project? Your job? Your finances? Your family members? Your friends? Try and notice those thoughts and scrutinize how important or how stressful they are for you. Then ask yourself about your worries, If it's going to happen, do you want it to happen?

Stress Diagram

Do you believe that someone or something is beyond us? The god? The super power? The one, who has the notes of our karma, will give the results according to our karma. Then what is the reason to be stressed out? Remember one thing if there's faith then there's no room for stress and fear, you do not ask for anything when you have faith in yourself, your karmas and the superpower you believe in. To ask for anything or to have any insatiable greed is not faith.You only need something to distract your mind from THAT one thing that you're constantly recalling and asking yourself to not remember it. If you can't find that something, the subconscious mind, in the process of forgetting it, will repeat those things and you will have that urge and will need some outer source (alcohol, smoking, whatever you need) to control or stop your thoughts for SOMETIME only. After that? Another day, same you, right? It's like you sleep late every night and then you apply the under eye cream everyday & expect your dark circles to vanish in a jiffy then that's not going to work. In order to heal yourself totally you need the inner treatment and not the outer source. The outer treatment is always temporary but the inner treatment is permanent.The treatment is within you.

> "*Fix the inputs and the outputs will fix themselves.*"

- **James Clear**

ᑭᑭᑭ

People want to be independent but they are bound by the trend of getting dependent. Why are you allowing anything to control yourself? Don't let anything control you, control your food intake, your thoughts, your habits. Take charge of your habits, human beings were never designed to be controlled by anything or anyone. We're given the ability to distinguish between the good and the bad. In order to look cool, in order to be a part of the party, people want to look a certain way, act a certain way, speak a certain way and that's where the originality is lost. It's so excruciating to see this happening around us everyday but can do nothing about it.

> "*We all have different question papers in life. Don't compare and don't copy.*"

- **Gaur Gopal Das**

ᑭᑭᑭ

You are here for a different purpose, that person is on this planet for another purpose, get influenced by how dedicated they are for their work, don't literally get influenced and imitate everything they do. They cannot always be perfect and aren't always doing the right things, if he's drinking alcohol or smoking cigarettes that doesn't mean you have to. Stop yourself from getting influenced by people's bad qualities and get influenced by their good qualities. Adopting some good things from others and duplicating them have a very thin line of difference which I am trying to highlight here &

requesting you to check the same on an individual, personal level.

TEN

HOW TO MULTIPLY YOUR WEALTH THROUGH THE RIGHT WAYS?

"If money and material things make you believe you are better than others, you are the poorest person on Earth."

If money had no value what would you do? Would you still do what you were doing right now? Would you still opt for that degree you're pursuing? Would you still do that 9 to 5 monotonous job that you're doing? Would you still continue that business because of which you're not getting the proper sleep and not giving your family the time they deserve with you? The value that money has, was only created for us so that we don't misuse or don't take granted for what we have. But what we did is that we made it such an important part of our life that whatever we're doing we're expecting money or some reward in return. When we do not get anything in return, we aren't convinced to do anything for anyone. Whatever is achieved, by giving someone pain, by hurting someone directly or indirectly, by stealing, by robbing does not ripe good fruits for you. Today or tomorrow you will repay all that. As they say, you cannot buy love & happiness. I believe you cannot buy a single thing with ONLY money. The way through which you're getting your money matters the most. If you're getting your money from the wrong way, you won't be able to digest that money. In the same way, if you've achieved your money by the right way but you're only using it for yourself, your family and not helping a single soul who's in need, then that money, in one way or the other will be snatched away from you and you won't even realise that. There are 2 ways through which you can multiply your wealth with the right path.

The first and foremost is, we are expected to give as much as we can, if we aren't doing that we're stopping the cycle of the flow of money in the universe. "**The law of Receiving**". To receive, you must give that which you wish to receive. The state of mind matters the most here. If you're holding onto your money, just because you're afraid of not paying the bills in the future, then which is the dominant state of mind here? The fear. And as I reiterate, fear and faith can never go hand in hand. Where fear exists it blocks the growth, because you prefer to stay in your comfort zone and comfort zone is a beautiful place to be in, because there's no change and so, there's no growth in there. Keep a note on where you spend your money, ask yourself every time you buy a new thing, can I live without this? Is this necessary? Can I buy it later and use this money for something else? If I won't buy this, will it be okay? Is this necessary right now? Can I buy anything else with this money that is more important to me? This won't make you a miser but this will allow you to think less of you and more of others. If you can donate generously then no need to ask these questions to yourself but if you think you don't have enough money to donate, you don't have enough guts. Yes, I used the word guts, because I have seen fat cats earning for their own and their families and arranging parties and big weddings for the sake of society's approval or can I use the word "show off"? Because when it comes to putting hands in their pockets for someone who's in need, they don't have enough money. I'm not asking here to be prodigal or to be selfless or not think about you & your family or not to spend your bucks on weddings and parties. Buy for yourself first, complete your priorities first, do your savings and then donate that amount in which you're comfortable in giving. Again, the intentions and emotions matter here. If you give just for the sake of giving and you're not happy while giving, it does not count. Don't give just for sake of it, give it because you want to make someone happy because you are blessed with the thing that others aren't. It's your responsibility. If you're not in a position to give someone something physically, give the most efficacious and helpful gift. Which I call - "silent gifts", the gift of blessings or a prayer or just being a good listener to someone who needs to be heard. All these gifts are way more precious than the physical & monetary gifts. This will cost you nothing but can matter to someone the most. You never know. So, whenever you step out of your house or even in your own house give silent gifts to everyone you come into contact with daily, any living being, any human. Because what we take for the other lives is these small deeds only. Not the money which you're congregating right now.

The second and the most avoided path by us is practising gratitude. The boring or I can say the not so important part of our lives. Whenever you pay a bill, a cheque, a payment, be thankful, be grateful that you got the money to pay your bills.Half a loaf is better than none, right? Stop incessantly talking about you have to pay the bills, you don't have enough money, you don't have enough of this, enough of that. You have everything that you should have. Be grateful for what you have right now, either it's money or your relations or anything in your life, stop complaining it sends the negative vibrations in the universe and you will always be psychologically in that state of "not getting enough". To get more, be thankful for what you already have right now, the feeling of satisfaction and happiness will instinctively generate good vibes within you and it will send a message in the universe that you're ready to receive more of it.The way you feel is the way you shape your life.

Epilogue

"*Without your past you could never have arrived, so wondrously and brutally... **here.***"

- **Taylor Swift**

ᑭᑭᑭ

I feel that in any era, any generation, in adulthood where we have the highest level of energy & time we spend it in having fun, adventure, experiencing new things and we want to achieve everything in our twenties and early thirties (and that's really not wrong at all). But with all those dreams we want to achieve, we should first try to know ourselves. We've made spirituality so boring that no one wants to indulge in it unless they're 60, when they're no good for anything else. Spirituality was never about chanting the name of god all day or fasting. The only purpose of fasting is to give your digestion system a break for sometime so it works well the next day. The only purpose of chanting God's name is to get peace of mind and have faith in something that is superior to us.

This book is purely based on my perception towards life, the perception which I've gained from my experiences, reading news articles, books like Bhagwat Geeta, Aptavani book, my parent's teachings & advice through years & my own thoughts and beliefs. These are my points of view for living a healthy, happy and contented life and a life towards **moksha**. If you agree with what I'm saying and if you find at least some of the answers for your questions then I am satisfied. Here, I would like to clear one last thing that be it the Geeta, the Quran, the Bible, the Agamas, the Tripitaka or any other holy book, they all teach us to be ONE. Every holy book teaches us to never hurt a single soul. We all are one, we all have come from the same energy. So, kindly stop wasting time on these stereotypical thinking and dividing human beings in the name of Dharma and start improving yourself on a daily basis.

You are impeccable. It's not that whatever is written in this book is unprecedented, you're OMNISCIENT but the only thing that's stopping you are your thoughts and your ignorance only.

The process is long. Learning, understanding, unlearning, making mistakes, learning the lessons. It's all a part of life that makes us unique (our experiences) and that, concisely, is known as GROWTH. Let us understand ourselves together.

Thank you for keeping the patience of reading the whole book. May god bless you with everything you want. May you all get moksha. Best wishes for your journey towards knowing yourself!

Acknowledgement

I would like to thank the universe for everything I have and for the people I have in my life, who supported me, encouraged me, taught me, scolded me, improved me and made me whoever I am right now. I am aware about the fact that this is not a milestone that I've achieved and I need to improve myself in so many areas but this certainly is the beginning of it. Special mentions to my parents for always guiding me whenever I was about to make a mistake (or did one). I'm blessed to have been born in a family like mine and the friends I have who are always available for me in every situation. Not to mention anyone's names here because they already know who they are. Thank you for choosing my work to read.

9 798886 064490

Printed by Libri Plureos GmbH in Hamburg,
Germany